1

# The Flowers That Opened

By

John C Burt.

There once was a sunflower that had been transplanted to the wilds of the British Isles, namely to the Scotland Highlands and a farm there ....

Now as you would know and understand sunflowers are called sunflowers because they love the sun .... they sort of follow the sun ...

Of course as you would know the weather on the Scottish Highlands in winter and even in autumn is anything but kind and even sunny ?

The sunflower's name was Alex ... and he was a beauty of a sunflower ... he had been raised in a greenhouse specifically for the task ..........

Winter and the cold , cold weather pressed in on the very Scottish Highlands .... even on the farm Alex the sunflower was planted in .... there was snow and sleet everywhere ..

Having come from the greenhouse and then suddenly being planted in the Highlands was a shock to the very and whole system of the sunflower called Alex ... He had never seen snow before .....

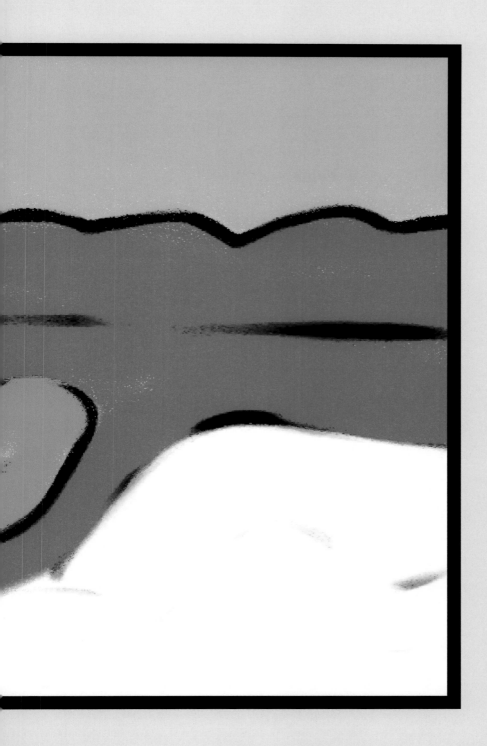

Alex the sunflower found himself wanting and thinking a lot about the very hot heat of the greenhouse ... Alex could get quite wistful .....

...when he had time to think about the past and his past life ... Alex's life now was made up of a lot of fresh, very fresh and very cold snow, ice and sleet .... If only it was not so cold !

Then ... one day
Alex found that
he could open his
petals , they were
a nice and pretty
shade of yellow,
much like the sun
he loved and
followed each
day .... each day.

Alex the sunflower was overjoyed , he could now spend his whole day and all of his days he hoped secretly following the hot , really hot sun in it's tracks across the sky ..........

Alex the sunflower ... literally bloomed and bloomed during the long days and the ever long twilight of the Northern Summer .........

Alex the sunflower was a completely different sunflower in the sun and the ever - increasing heat of the Northern Summer ......

For Alex the sunflower the cold winds of change and the Northern winter had long passed and he looked forward to more and more and much more heat and endless sun and summer days ..

Alex the sunflower was truly a sunflower ... he loved the sun and it's heat but did not think too much at all of winter and it's snow and ice everywhere ...Alex hoped to follow the sun all the days of his life ....